THE POET HEROIC

The Kota Series Companion Story

Sunshine Somerville

This is a work of fiction. Similarities to real people, places, or events are entirely coincidental.

THE POET HEROIC

First edition. December 25, 2015.

ISBN: 979-8230824152

Written by Sunshine Somerville.

Table of Contents

Books by Sunshine Somerville

The Kota Series

The Prophet in the Hoodie: Intro to The Kota Series
The Kota
The Ebonite and Her Earthling
Pharmakon
Zenith Prophecies
The Woman of the Void
The Poet Heroic

The Alt-World Chronicles

The Eighth: Intro to The Alt-World Chronicles
Alterni
Malevolenci
Origini
The Fairy Master Capturi
Sirens and Assassi
Deus Endi

A Fairly Fairy Tale

See more at
SunshineSomerville.com

In Loving Memory of

Jeff
and for anyone else struggling to find the light.

Dominion Newsfeed

07/08/69 22:00
Paris, Crow's Region, Mainland-Euro
– ALERT: Unauthorized Streaming Video Upload
...Tracking coordinates...

The room is dark. A wall of windows allows faint city light to stretch into the room, but the light only reaches far enough to reveal a skyscraper's vacant office space.

A spotlight turns on to reveal a man in his late twenties sitting in a chair. His head is lowered so that his coat's hood shields his face from the camera. He sits comfortably, his hands in his lap.

In a chair across from him sits a stylish woman with neon green hair. This is Kaytrine Elique, known rebel hacker-turned-reporter. A Euro woman who speaks only an illegal language, she wears a headset translating device. She also holds a paper notepad presumably filled with questions. With a smirk, she turns her head and looks into the camera.

Her headset translates in her own accented voice as she says, "We know we don't have much time before this transmission is tracked by the monitors. And I have no doubt the Dominion is very interested to know the location of my guest tonight. His name is Vale Olander. Or as most of us know him, Beathabane. The Forgotten Son. The Tyrant Twin. So, without wasting any more time, let's hear what my guest has to say." She turns to the man in the chair. "Sir, thank you for agreeing to this interview."

The man now lifts his hood from his head and pushes it back to reveal his face.

Kaytrine sucks in breath at the sight of him, but she regains her composure immediately. "I'm sorry, but you look exactly-"

"I know," Beathabane tells her with a smile. "You're not the first to have that reaction." He glances at the camera nervously, then to the side, where he probably has a man positioned for security.

"I'll get right to it," Kaytrine tells him as she examines her notes. "Everyone knows the work you've been doing this past decade since..." She makes a face. "Since you came to the Mainland. You've helped scores of refugees. Saved hundreds of lives. But this is the first time you've agreed to publically speak out. Why is that?"

"I thought it was about time to show my pretty face," Beathabane jokes. Then he takes a deep breath and sits up in his chair. "Like you say, people know the work I've done with my team. They've heard rumors about me, both from the Dominion and the rebels. I want my supporters to see my face and know for certain that I'm still alive. And I want those who distrust me to know that I'm not my twin. I want everyone to know that I'll never stop working to make this world a better place for all of us. That's all I want. People have no need to fear me. And I hope my example will prompt others to join us in this fight for what is right and just."

Kaytrine taps her notepad. "As the first reporter you've been willing to speak to, I have to ask – what about your sister?"

Beathabane flinches in his seat, and his jaw tightens.

Kaytrine glances at the camera. "Everyone is wondering, you know. Your brother brought her into the Dominion not long after you came to the Mainland. Since then, she's been learning to fight for the very things you're fighting against. I have to wonder if that makes you view her as an enemy. And if not, how can you live with the fact that your sister is in the Dominion's care? I would think, sir, that you'd do everything in your power to rescue her. Or am I wrong?"

Beathabane pauses in thought. Then he looks back at Kaytrine calmly to answer.

1

The Capitol House

Vale knew he wasn't his father's favorite son. Knew – not suspected. There were downsides to being a telepath.

"He's just like his mother," was a thought that often went through his father's mind when he wasn't pleased with Vale. Considering Vale remembered little of his mother but knew his father quite well, Vale chose to see this comparison as a compliment.

Sharing a room with his twin brother while they were children had been his father's idea of making a man out of him. Vale had always been more interested in literature and philosophy; Cruelthor was drawn to war strategy and business. Both boys had thrilled their tutors with a natural aptitude for historical application, and Vale had many happy memories of touring historical sites while they'd been children on the Mainland-Euro. But their father wanted them to follow in his rule, and so they'd moved to the Northern Continent to live in the Capitol House and focus their studies on Dominion government.

Now eighteen, Vale had his own quarters. His study room was purposefully free of distractions, though all his rooms in the Capitol House were simple and clean. He'd always preferred to read out of paper books rather than a terminal screen, and three books lay open atop his oak desk now. He was studying the history of the DRK, an ancient virus that had nearly eliminated the human race before the original Dominion leader discovered a treatment.

It's sick, thought Vale as he looked at ancient pictures of quarantined and infected citizens. This is the Dominion practice I disagree with most. We should give the DRK treatment to everyone, worldwide, and wipe out this virus once and for all. The Dominion has enough power without needing to use the virus as a weapon against our enemies. And the infected factors that roam the unsettled regions are dangerous if not put down. We should protect our citizens.

Vale got up from his desk and went to his door. Out in the second-story hall, he was immediately struck by the splendor of the Capitol House, the seat of power for the ruling Dominion leader, his father, Thurston Olander. A sparkling chandelier hung over the open room beyond the hall's railing. Portraits of past Dominion rulers lined the hall, but Vale chose to watch his steps over the plush red carpet. When he reached the stairs, Vale looked out a window to see the green lawns of the garden, and the perfect fall day called to him.

I need a break from studying, he thought. Final exams or no, I'm going out.

The base of the stairs met the open room under the chandelier, and Vale heard his father's voice shouting from an office not far away. Vale always knew who his father was talking to depending on his tone. A modicum of respect meant he was talking to his Elite governors or commanders. Complete distain meant he was addressing one of the Capitol House servants. Pride meant he was talking to Cruelthor. Barely veiled annoyance and anger meant he was talking to Vale.

Now, the Lord High Commander was shouting at Commander Rilen, which was abnormal. "Rilen, I don't care how many men you sent! If they didn't find her, send more!"

A door slammed.

Vale darted across the open room to a side door. Here, he entered a mud room with very un-Dominion, untidy piles of yard tools. Vale found his smelly running shoes tucked in a corner behind a bag of birdseed, and he quickly put them on before reaching for the exterior door.

Outside, he paused on the step and took in a breath of crisp fall air. He descended the steps and started jogging up the path that would lead deeper into the gardens. The lawn was pristine. The fountains were clean, not a stray leaf floating on their surfaces. The pebbled footpath he ollowed crunched under his feet, and the rhythmic sound of his steps rought him some comfort and familiarity. The cold breeze blowing into is hair and against his warming body felt wonderful.

Rounding a bend of tall bushes, however, Vale slowed his pace when e saw his brother playing a ballgame with some friends. The boys were ll classmates from the Dominion Youth program. All were strapping hysical specimens. All bore personality traits common to nultiple-generation loyalists – they were arrogant, spoiled, unkind by earned behavior and habit.

"Beathabane!" his brother called. Cruelthor stopped play and waved 'ale onto the field.

The other boys didn't argue, but when they looked at Vale he felt vaves of *contempt* and *respect* radiate from their minds in equal measure.

"Hey, Beathabane," said a muscular, dark-skinned young man a little horter than Vale and Cruelthor's height.

"Hi, Troubogaust," Vale answered politely. He never argued their use f his father's nickname for him. There would be no point. But in his wn mind, he still thought of himself as Vale – the name his mother had iven him.

"Play with us," said Cruelthor.

Vale wavered.

"Oh, come on," said Cruelthor with an I-can-win-you-over grin. He cked Vale the ball. "Clearly you're done studying if you came out here run. Join us."

Vale rolled the ball with his foot, testing the air pressure. He smiled. Okay. But only until the first goal."

The other boys were satisfied with this and returned to their ositions on the field. Cruelthor gave Vale a playful shoulder slap, which as harder than it would've been a few years earlier...

While Vale was secretly a telepath, his twin brother had a very fferent skill set. Their father had had them tested when they turned n to see if they carried mutate-genes, but only Cruelthor's tests were positive. For the next few years, the talk of the land had focused o guessing what Cruelthor's mutate-genetic abilities might turn out t be. Then came puberty, and Cruelthor's mutate-genes had kicked i enhancing his strength tenfold. It had been a dangerous time to be hi younger twin, and Vale had been careful not to piss him off. Val meanwhile, developed the ability to hear other people's thoughts, spea in their minds, and sense their feelings. This had been a complete surpris and freaked Vale out at first, but he was glad he could hide his gift an avoid the attention Cruelthor's strength received from the public.

Vale kicked the ball to his brother, and together they raced for th other end of the field. Vale was faster – at least he had that. Cruelthor cu left around a defender, passed the ball to a teammate, and Vale ran int position to score.

Suddenly, a loud shout cut through the game's commotion. "Wh in the name of the Twenty-Five Regions do you boys think you' doing?"

Everyone stopped running and looked over to see Command Guown, the Youth program's History instructor, on the edge of the fiel The big man stood with his arms crossed. He didn't look pleased.

The whole herd of boys jogged off the field and scrambled to star at attention before the commander.

Guown stroked his sandy mustache and let out a huff. His Eu accent grew thick with his anger. "Three days until final exams, and yo knuckleheads think it's a good time to play football? If every single o of you doesn't get your butts back to your desks in the next half hour, I' going to report to your fathers if you do not absolutely ace my sectio exams!" He raised an eyebrow at Vale in particular.

"You can't afford to give your father room for criticism, lad," he though knowing Vale could hear his thoughts through a mind link Vale h created a long time ago. There were few people Vale fully trusted, b Guown was one of them.

Vale nodded slightly at his teacher.

Guown took a step into Cruelthor's face. "Especially you! I expect you to be a better leader by now. Set an example, heir. Hop to!"

"Yes, sir!" Cruelthor saluted and turned to his friends. "You heard the commander!"

The boys took off in different directions across the gardens, each heading for their quarters. Vale jogged with his brother, matching him stride for stride.

"I'm going to gut that old man when we take over." Cruelthor laughed.

Vale smiled, hoping his brother was kidding.

An hour later, Vale slipped out of his room and walked down the hall to his brother's beautiful oak door. Knocking, Vale heard his brother think him inside.

He walked in to find Cruelthor not at his desk but sitting on his sofa. His feet rested on his coffee table. His hands worked a controller to the game console operating the holo-screen that covered the far wall. A live-action battle scene lit up this wall, and Cruelthor was running his avatar through a minefield while shooting bloodied, fungus-covered factor monsters infected with the DRK virus.

Vale shivered, never comfortable seeing factors even in holographic form.

"What's up?" asked Cruelthor. He pointed to the other controller on the table. "Jump in."

Vale sat on the sofa beside his twin and took the controller, activated his avatar, and started shooting the factors running toward them. "You finish studying?"

"Nope. Taking a break."

"I figured." Vale shot a factor about to bite into Cruelthor's avatar.

"Thanks." Cruelthor moved his whole body to help the controller do his bidding as his avatar ran around a corner. "You really think exams are going to be that hard?"

"Well, they're our Youth finals, so yeah. For everyone else, the exams just mean getting assigned executive or operative status, so I guess I can see why Troubogaust doesn't care. But you and I'll be officially prepared to govern the Dominion after this. We'll have to know our stuff to prove we're not just coddled brats."

Cruelthor scoffed. "We're not coddled."

You are, thought Vale. You don't bother to study. You mouth off all the time. But no one yells at you. It's not because they're afraid of your strength either. They're afraid of Dad. ...Everyone's afraid of Dad, lately.

Vale hit pause on his game. This was the real reason he'd come to see his brother. They were close – maybe not as close as twins were supposed to be, but they were close. If Vale was having concerns about their father, he was sure Cruelthor was too.

"Have you seen Dad today?" asked Vale. "He's been really punchy."

Cruelthor frowned but didn't pause his game. "Yeah, he yelled at the cook this morning and called her Vedanleé. Accused her of trying to poison him. Weird."

"Exactly. He's been really weird the past few days. I heard some of the commanders talking. They think Dad is cursed. By..."

Cruelthor laughed. "Vedanleé? They really believe Mom cursed him?"

Vale nodded, slightly embarrassed. "You don't think it's possible? I mean, we studied our genealogy when we lived on the Mainland-Euro. All that with the Kota camp in the north... Those people were supposedly witches, Cruelthor. I once heard an Elite governor thinking that maybe Dad's own grandmother cursed him a long time ago. We know Dad snapped and killed all of them once we were born, so maybe..."

Now Cruelthor paused the game and looked at him with mockery. "You and your head voodoo. Dad is cracking up, I'll admit, but blaming it on magic is a little nuts."

Vale looked down at the controller in his hands. "You're not a little curious about Mom?"

"We haven't seen her since we picked our noses, so who cares?"

"When I heard the commanders talking, they said something about Mom showing up a few days ago."

"What? Why weren't we told?"

"I don't know. The commanders seemed really freaked out. Angry." He looked at his brother. "They said she took a squadron of drone soldiers with her when she left. Why would Dad let her do that? And it was around then that Dad started acting so crazy. Maybe she really was here and...cursed him."

Cruelthor thought a minute and made a face. "Or, maybe *she* poisoned him, not the cook. There's always a reasonable explanation."

Someone knocked on the door.

Cruelthor, annoyed, rolled his eyes and called, "Come in!"

A servant opened the door and bowed. "Sir, your father requests your presence for a private dinner."

Cruelthor shut down the game and rose from the couch. "Alright, fine. I'm hungry anyway. Better not be duck again."

Vale also stood.

"Uh," the servant stammered. "Just Cruelthor. The Lord High Commander requested only Cruelthor for dinner."

Not surprised, Vale turned to his brother and shrugged. "Guess I'll finish studying."

The next morning, one of Vale's mind links woke him early. A feeling of *wrong* radiated into Vale's mind, strong enough to make him open his eyes.

It was Commander Guown's mind-voice he heard. *"You need to get to your father, lad. Quickly. He's dying. I'm sorry."*

Vale swallowed. *"I'll be right there."*

He quickly went to his closet and dressed in clothes his father approved of. Then he hurried out his door.

Down on the main floor, servants stood in groups, whispering. A few commanders near his father's wing of the Capitol House watched Vale as he trotted over.

"I thought Cruelthor already... Oh, that's the other one."

"The Lord High Commander was asking for trouble, dealing with that woman."

Vale ignored them and entered his father's hall, then slowed as he approached his father's door. A servant here saw him coming, opened the door, and stood to the side with his head bowed.

Inside his father's dimly lit bedroom, Vale found a small crowd. Most were his father's trusted commanders, including Guown, who met Vale's eyes and gave the boy an encouraging smile. Then Vale saw Cruelthor standing near their father's headboard. Cruelthor's expression told Vale everything – their father was dying. Vale walked to join his twin, and together they looked down at their father.

Thurston Olander was thinner than he'd ever been, his face gaunt and pale. His golden hair was stuck to his sweaty forehead. His eyes swung from Cruelthor to Vale and back again.

"These are my sons," he said hoarsely. He coughed and lifted his hand to grasp Cruelthor's wrist. "I name Cruelthor sole heir to the Dominion throne. Upon my death, he will be Lord High Commander of the Dominion Empire. All authority passes to him..." He choked and fought for air.

A nurse stepped to the bed and tended to him.

Vale glanced at the commanders and saw them shuffling and looking at each other, then at him. He looked away.

I shouldn't be surprised by this, he thought. I'm... I'm not surprised. t would be too complicated for us both to rule. Cruelthor is more suited or it than I am, anyway. ...Dad's probably always planned this.

Not wanting to know his brother's thoughts at the moment, Vale still ensed a wave of emotions. *Confusion. Anger. Excitement.*

Then, Cruelthor's thoughts were too strong not to hear. *"Everything ather told me last night is unreal! How could he hide this from me until ow! No wonder he slaughtered our people! And now Mom's escaped again. ad's a goner. I'm going to have to clean up this mess."*

Vale looked away.

What the hell? he thought. What is going on?

"Find her!" Thurston shouted suddenly. He shoved the nurse away nd looked around the room, his eyes not focusing on any of them. She betrayed me! I killed them. I killed them all. But her – find her! he girl must not live! She must not live! The prophecy! She will ruin verything!"

Vale looked at Cruelthor, who seemed to understand whatever their ther was babbling about.

"Vedanleé..." Thurston stopped moving. His mouth hung open. His yes did not blink.

The nurse checked him, then looked at the twins. "I'm sorry. He's one."

Cruelthor didn't even take a pause. He turned to the commanders. end the techs to the command office immediately. I want my ID tag programmed to access my father's files." With that, he marched out of e room.

Vale looked down at their father, then after his departed brother.

What the hell? he thought again.

ruelthor had insisted upon an immediate cremation of their father's dy, followed by an afternoon service with hundreds of the Dominion's most loyal citizens in attendance. The commanders and local governo had all expressed condolences to their new ruler, and Cruelthor had bee surrounded by them all day.

Vale, on the other hand, spent the day alone. The onl acknowledgements anyone had given him were uncertain glances and few kind words of sympathy. Now in his sitting room, he rested with a open fiction book on his lap.

They don't know what to do with me, he thought. To be honest, don't know what to do with me. Dad is dead... Why am I not sadd about that? He was a jerk, but he was my father. What am I feelin Relief? I feel relief. I don't have to be a Dominion High Commander. can be... What do I want to be?

He jumped in his seat when he heard his door open. Cruelth strode in, lifted his eyebrows at Vale, and sat in the chair facing him. H wore his finest clothes, the same he'd wore at the funeral service earlie He sat in the chair with a new level of authority.

Already, thought Vale. He's already accepted all of this.

"Greetings, Lord High Commander," said Vale with a bob of h head.

Cruelthor tried to hide a grin. "I thought I'd better come speak wi you and make sure there weren't any hard feelings. I honestly had no id until last night that Dad was planning this."

"So he told you last night?" Vale was finally able to ask the questio he'd had all day. "What else did he tell you? Do you know what he w talking about, there at the end?"

Cruelthor picked a stray hair off his sleeve with a frown. "He to me a lot of things, Beathabane. A lot of it is...confidential. But now h ravings lately make sense. I'll tell you what I can, but... There are son Dominion secrets that are for me alone to know. No offense."

Vale nodded, trying to adjust to this new dynamic.

"What was Dad saying about Mom? Did you learn anything abo that?"

"Yeah." Cruelthor scratched his chin. "All of that is actually why I'm here. I knew you'd want to know. And I need your help."

"Okay?"

"Mom did come back a few days ago. Turns out, she was in hiding with a group of our Kota people this whole time. She had a new husband and a daughter. A whole happy, new family."

Vale sat back in surprise. He didn't know what he'd expected to hear, but... Their mother had made a new life and been happy?

"A little while ago," Cruelthor went on, "I guess her new husband made her angry or something, and she tried to run away with their daughter. But the guy kept their kid and sent Mom away on her own. That's why Mom came back here. Considering Dad wanted her and all the Kota dead, that seems pretty stupid. But, I guess she was desperate to get her daughter back. She made a deal with Dad. She told him she'd lead his soldiers to the Kota remnant she'd been living with so the soldiers could slaughter them. In exchange, she wanted Dad to promise he'd allow her and her daughter to live in peace."

Vale, amazed, wiped his face with his hands. "I'm guessing Dad didn't do that."

"Nope. Commander Rilen took a whole squadron of drone soldiers to where Mom and the girl were living, and his orders were to kill her on sight. But Mom must've not trusted Dad – guess she's not so stupid after all – and she wasn't there when Rilen showed up. She's vanished. Again."

Vale nodded in thought. "So did Mom curse Dad? She must've known he wouldn't keep his promise, so she cursed him."

Cruelthor rolled his eyes. "If anything, maybe she poisoned him."

There's no point arguing about it, thought Vale. Whatever happened, Dad's dead. Mom is gone again.

This was all so crazy, but one thing made his heart a little lighter. "We have a little sister?" He smiled at his twin.

"Half-sister, yeah."

"Right before Dad died, he said to kill them. He said, 'The girl must not live.' So..." He swallowed but was relieved to see Cruelthor shaking his head.

"No, I'm not going to kill our little sister. I can't tell you everything, but I know what Dad was so afraid of. I know why he killed our Kota people. He was nuts, but he had his reasons." Cruelthor bit his lip in thought. "But I don't think our sister is a threat. At least, not yet. If we can get to her first, we can bring her here to live with us."

Vale nodded in agreement.

Thank God, he thought. This poor girl...

"How old is she? Any idea where she is?"

"She's six, as far as we can sort out. And nope – no idea where she is. That's where you come in." Cruelthor leaned forward and raised an eyebrow. "I'm being publically named Lord High Commander next week, so I need all the time I can get between now and then to plan my coronation ceremony."

Yet we buried Dad in an afternoon, thought Vale.

"Once I'm in charge," Cruelthor went on, "I'll have a ton of work on my plate. I don't and won't have time to find our sister. But..."

"But I do." Vale nodded. "I'll talk to Commander Rilen and go to Mom's last known whereabouts. I'll look for clues. Maybe someone knows where she went."

"What makes you think anyone would tell you?"

Vale smirked. "What makes you think they'll have to?"

Cruelthor matched his smirk. "Good point." He rose from his chair. "I'll bump up your usual security detail and give you one of Dad's...one of my private jets. Check in with me if you find anything."

"Will do."

"I'll see you next week for my coronation?"

"Wouldn't miss it." Vale smiled awkwardly.

As the door closed behind his brother, Vale rose to pack a bag.

2

Vancouver

He hadn't been in the woods for years, certainly not since moving to the Capitol House. Not like this. Not in the wild.

The hiking trail had thinned several kilometers ago. He now stepped over frosted roots and rocks, his boots crunching the crisp fall leaves. Branches stretched over the trail, and he'd ordered his bodyguards not to disrupt the foliage. Brom led him while Tor and Coi followed behind, guns at the ready.

He'd searched for six days. The house his mother supposedly had lived in was empty. The Kota camp the Dominion drones had attacked was a dead end of information – burned corpses and piles of destruction were all that remained. The closest population in Vancouver reported hearing heavy gunfire in the woods, but understandably no one had investigated. Shortly thereafter, a few local grocers said a woman and young girl had been around, shopping for food and supplies before disappearing into the woods again.

She's out here in the wilderness somewhere, thought Vale. *They* are. When I find them-

A gunshot sounded, echoing over the wild terrain.

"Ugh!" Brom suddenly doubled over and fell against a tree.

"Brom?" Vale hurried forward, pushing aside a branch. "What-"

Another gunshot.

Vale ducked and sank to his knees beside Brom, who winced and held his bleeding chest.

"Beathabane!" Tor called from behind.

Vale looked back and saw Tor and Coi running to him, guns raised as they scanned the trees.

"He's hit!" Vale called. He looked back at Brom. "Hold on, they're-"

More gunshots.

Tor fell first, hit in the leg. He got off a shot before another bullet found his chest. Then he lay still on the ground, bleeding out. Coi ran three more strides before a perfect shot struck his head, and he fell straight forward, never to move again.

"Beathabane, run!" Brom ordered. He grabbed Vale's jacket to look at him. His eyes were wide and stern. "Run!"

Five more gunshots erupted in quick succession, one bullet ricocheting off the tree beside Vale's head.

"Go, kid! They're here to slay you! Go!"

Vale looked around, saw a clear path behind him, and checked his fallen bodyguards one last time. Then he jumped to his feet and ran through the woods. Gunshots fired, and he tensed before realizing he wasn't hit. He ran harder, pushing through branches and choosing his footing as best he could. More gunshots fired, now from the opposite direction. They didn't seem focused on him, but he didn't stop to investigate. He ran uphill and over to find an open clearing with an abandoned cabin in the center.

Cover, he thought. Get to cover.

He sprinted across the clearing and reached the cabin. The steps of the porch were broken, but he jumped over them and landed on the porch, which fortunately didn't collapse under him. The cabin door hung loose on its hinges, and he pulled it open while trying to hold it intact. Once through, he wedged the door shut again before turning to see where he was.

A window on either side of the room allowed light into the abandoned building. Dirt covered the floor. A chunk of the ceiling hung down. A dark area on the far side of the room looked like it might lead into a hall.

Gunshots from some distance away echoed through the woods.

Vale turned back to the door and closed one eye to look outside hrough a crack.

"Don't freak out, okay?" said a female voice.

Vale whipped around and looked to the dark hall. He'd been panting efore, but now he found his throat was dry. "Who... Who's there?"

Footfalls came first, and then a young woman stepped out of the hadowed hall, her arms raised. She came into the light from the indows, and Vale saw she was about his own age. She wore boots, hermal pants, and a slick dark coat. Her head was shaved except for a raided mohawk of blond hair, the ponytail of which was pulled over her houlder. Her blue eyes widened as she smiled at him.

"Hello, Beathabane."

"What is going on? Who are you?"

"I need you to calm down, okay? I'll explain everything." She kept er hands raised.

Vale looked out the windows, sure that guns would poke inside and m at him any minute.

"The Underground sent assassins," said the girl. "That's who shot our men. My team is trying to scare them off. We've got this cabin urrounded, so don't worry. We won't let the Underground get you."

The Underground, thought Vale.

He knew of the rebel group. They were the strongest opposition to he Dominion, attacking bases and committing crimes all over the globe.

"They're trying to kill me?"

The girl blinked. "Well, yeah."

He tried to think. "Your team? Who are you? Are you operatives? id Cruelthor send an extra team to protect-"

"No." The girl shook her head. "Sweetie, I'm not Dominion. But I n here to help you."

"Why should I believe you?" Vale felt for the door behind him, but didn't see how he could make a quick escape that way.

She smiled and lifted an eyebrow. "Read my mind."

He froze. "What are you talking about?"

"You're a telepath. It's a big secret, but... I know." She smiled agai "Go ahead. The easiest way for me to prove you can trust me is to let yo look in my mind."

Vale wavered. If he distracted himself by looking in her mind, she have time to attack him. "How do you know about my telepathy?"

"We'll get to that. Just go ahead and read my mind, Little Lor Fauntleroy."

He made a face. "In no way am I like-"

"Crap, no, that's totally off, isn't it? Literature was never really m thing, but I was trying to impress you. I was always way better at Scienc and Math." She winked. "You're not the only one with a Dominio education, you know."

"I thought you're not Dominion."

Her face grew serious for the first time. "Not anymore, I'm not." Sh tapped the side of her head. "Come on, telepath. Get on with it."

Vale hadn't heard shooting in a while. He was either completely o of danger or about to be in a lot more of it.

But I need to know what's going on, he thought.

He met her eyes, felt for her mind, and entered her thoughts.

She sneaks out of her parents' house and runs to a hovercar whe her friends are waiting. They cruise down the night streets until they g to a Dominion treatment station. Here, they park a short distance aw and hold back giggling as they quietly approach the station's side windou Peeking inside, they see a long line of poor citizens. She giggles with h friends to see the old clothes the citizens are wearing, and they point a laugh from outside the window. Then, as the last citizen in line receives h treatment injection from the Dominion doctors, one of the doctors ord drone soldiers to block the people from leaving. The citizens look arou in confusion and panic, and suddenly one bolts for the exit. The near drone shoots the citizen in the chest, and the man falls to the ground in puddle of blood. The girl and her friends stop laughing and watch as dron bring a giant cage into the room and push the citizens inside. The citizens cry and scream in terror, but the Dominion doctors ignore them as they stand before the cage. Then, one of the citizens falls to his knees and starts shaking. The others in the cage back away, but then another man starts convulsing and falls to the floor. Then another. Soon, every citizen in the cage is factoring from DRK infection. The girl then realizes that they weren't given treatment injections – they were directly injected with the virus. The citizens begin to shriek and growl, factoring as the DRK quickly evolves them into subhuman monsters. The girl and her friends back away from the station and run to their hovercar.

Vale closed his eyes and disconnected from her mind. He took a moment to analyze all he'd seen. Looking back at her, he saw she was unnerved by the memory she'd shared. *Regret*, *sorrow*, *shame*, and *rage* wafted from her mind.

"You're Nocturna," he said first, "Elite Sonne's daughter who went missing. The official report was that you were kidnapped by the Underground in retaliation for Sonne raising taxes on his region."

She shut down her emotions. "I know. I read the newsfeeds – which maybe you should do more of, by the way."

"I always keep up to datc on-"

"I don't mean that Dominion bullshit. I mean the rebel newsfeeds that report what's actually going on in the world. Seriously, Beathabane – I know what it's like to grow up in the Youth and think you know everything, but it's much smarter to wake up and learn the truth."

Vale opened his mouth to argue but closed it again as he remembered her memories.

I had no idea the Dominion was experimenting with the DRK, he thought. Those poor people. I know my father was doing some terrible things, but this...

"Now, as for why I'm here..." Nocturna took a step forward to peer up at him. "There's a lot you could do to help us."

"Us who? Who are you working for?"

"I'm with a new group of rebels. The Underground won't take us because they think we still have loyalties to the Dominion." She shook her head, *sincerity* radiating right off her. "But it's exactly because we were in the Dominion that we can do the most damage. We know how the system works. We have professional training. We're educated way more than the average citizen. And you..." She lifted her hands to point at him. "Imagine what you could do from the inside. You could help us end the Dominion once and for all!"

"End the-" Vale managed a laugh. "Are you kidding me? I'm not going to help you rebels bring down the only world order!"

She visibly forced herself not to yell at him, and she took a breath. "You're the one who likes stories. Do you know the one about the man in the iron mask?"

He swallowed, starting to see where this was going. "It's based on reports that an unknown man was imprisoned for decades under the rule of Louis XIV. There are several old legends and theories about who he was."

"And I think you know the theory I mean."

"Yeah, okay. An ancient storyteller suggested that the prisoner was the twin brother of Louis XIV. Louis ordered him to wear an iron mask so no one would know who he was. Louis didn't want his twin challenging his rule." Vale made a face at her. "What's your point?"

"The story goes that the man in the iron mask did escape and take Louis's place, ruling for years as a good king. You look just like the soon-to-be Lord High Commander. Think of the orders you could give if you posed as him! If you can get to Cruelthor and..."

"He'll never kill his own brother," she thought.

He leaned back into the door and glared at her. "I will not! Okay, I need to look into a few things and stop certain Dominion programs. Maybe I can change a few laws, make things easier for the citizens. Now that my father's gone, I'll end as much of his corruption as I can."

I've wanted to fix the Dominion system for a long time anyway, he thought.

"I will do *something* from the inside," he told her. "I promise. I'll do what I can to fix things. Maybe I can convince Cruelthor-"

Now Nocturna laughed. "You're a freakin' telepath! How do you not know your own brother?"

"What are you talking about?"

A man's voice yelled from the dark hall. "Your brother is your father's son!"

Vale knew the voice. He looked beyond Nocturna as a man emerged from the shadows.

Commander Guown sighed at Vale. "Oh, lad. I was hoping you'd listen to her."

"What are you doing here? You're with her?"

Nocturna took a step to the side and went silent. *Respect* overtook her whole demeanor.

"We don't have time for long explanations, lad. Your bodyguards are dead, and their ID tags will send a signal back to headquarters. Reinforcements will be here soon to retrieve you."

Good, thought Valc.

He looked down at his hand where his own ID tag was implanted.

Guown might've seen Vale's relief, and he said urgently, "You need to listen. The girl's right. The world is in serious trouble, and you can do something about it. But not the way you think – your brother is in charge of the kingdom now, and I guarantee he won't let you change things from the inside. But that doesn't mean you can't change things." Guown radiated *affection*. "You aren't like Cruelthor. I know that. I've always had faith in you, lad. I convinced these people that you're worth saving."

"You set this up? What are you doing with her?"

"I'm the new leader of her rebel group, since your brother tried to slay me five days ago."

Vale blinked. "What?"

"He's never liked me, and you know it. As soon as he had the authority, he ordered drones to slit me open old-school torture style. I got wind of it and ran for my life." He pulled off a glove and held out a freshly bandaged hand to show Vale. "I had to cut my ID tag out myself so the monitors can't track me."

Vale's head was spinning. "You became a rebel?"

Guown scoffed. "Come on, lad. You're smarter than that."

Now Vale understood. "You've always been a rebel."

Guown nodded. "A friend and I've helped Youth kids escape for years. The Dominion killed him a few days ago during a mission. Now I'm all these kids have left. As soon as I escaped your brother, I flew to their hideout on the Mainland. But now we've come back for you."

Ignoring this last bit, Vale shook his head in amazement. "How did you hide it from me? We have a mind link!" Then he understood and looked at Nocturna. "Guown, you told her I'm a telepath?"

"Yes," the big man answered bluntly. "As for how I hid things from you, your father actually helped with that. There's a telepath called Counterstrike who taught your instructors how to block telepathy. Your father was afraid of you digging around in our minds where you didn't belong."

Vale thought back. "That's why I couldn't always see in Dad's mind. He was blocking me."

"Yeah. That old bastard had a lot of secrets. When you became a telepath, I think it freaked him out for all kinds of reasons."

Vale felt his heart breaking. "This Counterstrike guy trained Cruelthor too, didn't he?"

"I'm sorry, lad. I'm afraid so. Your brother's been keeping things from you for a long time."

Nocturna cleared her throat.

Guown nodded at her and rested his bandaged hand on Vale's shoulder. "We don't have a lot of time. Nocturna's shown you a bit f how the Dominion abuses its power and hides the truth. And they o much, much worse. I know you think you can change things as ;ruelthor's brother, but he won't let you. Cruelthor doesn't want to ıake the Dominion less oppressive – he wants to make it worse. You eed to understand that. And you need to make a decision. Are you with s or the Dominion?"

"With you or my brother, you mean? I'm sorry, Guown, but I have › believe I can talk sense into Cruelthor. Together, we could fix-"

"How can you be so blind?" Nocturna apparently couldn't stay quiet ny longer. "Don't you know your brother is dancing in your father's ›otsteps? He could be the worst Olander yet!"

"I have to try!" Vale shouted back. He looked at Guown. "Please, you ave to let me try. Even if I can't get through to Cruelthor, maybe *I* can x some of the corruption from the inside." He thought of Nocturna's roposal. "But without killing my brother."

Guown sighed and shook his head. "This is a bad idea. But okay."

Nocturna gaped. "Sir!"

"We can't force him to join us," the big man argued. He looked Vale again. "Okay, lad. Better run back to your fallen bodyguards. 'e ran off the Underground assassins, so you'll be safe. Dominion inforcements should be here soon to rescue you."

Vale let out a breath. "Thank you."

"And please," added Guown, "don't tell them we met."

Vale's thoughts were impossible to sort out just yet, but... "I'll just say at I ran here to hide and went back when the shooting stopped."

"Thank you, lad."

Then Vale remembered why he was out here in the wilderness in the st place. "Oh, do you have any idea where my mom or sister are?"

"No. Sorry. But maybe you're beginning to understand that Vedanleé hiding from the Dominion for good reason."

Vale thought on this but could only nod. He turned for the door. I was stuck, but he tugged and shoved a few times before the old woo gave way.

"I'll keep an eye out for you," Guown called after him. "If you nee anything..."

"Yeah," said Vale. "Thanks."

With that, he hurried out of the cabin and down the steps. The col air iced his lungs as he took off running back the way he'd come.

3

Capital City

"I want to see my brother," Vale demanded.

The drone soldiers, mindless and programmed, ignored him. They stood with their backs to him outside his holding cell's force field gate.

Upon his return to the Capitol House, Vale had learned from Commander Rilen's mind that Cruelthor had indeed ordered him to kill Guown. Vale hadn't had time for further investigation, however. Cruelthor had summoned him to Capital City, where they'd begun construction of a new compound, and the Dominion seat of government had already shifted north, to this new location. Flown into Capital City by private jet, Vale had only arrived that morning. He'd already seen enough to worry his brother would drain the bank of kronar with his construction plans.

But that was before Dominion solders had arrested Vale and taken him to this prison cell.

What is going on? he thought.

Vale sat in his cell for some time before he heard the door at the end of the hall open. Footsteps marched down the corridor, and at last Cruelthor came to stand outside his cell. Vale examined his brother's fine clothes and suspected that he'd just arrived from his coronation ceremony.

"Cruelthor, what's going on?" Vale rose from his bench and stood as close to the force field as he dared. "I was on my way to your ceremony when Troubogaust-"

"I ordered Troubogaust to arrest you and hold you here for your protection," said Cruelthor. He stood with his hands clasped. His hair was slicked back, and his chiseled face looked quite stern as he looked down his nose at Vale.

"My protection?"

"Yes. Well, yours and mine. It seems a rebel team of assassins was discovered trying to get past security at my coronation ceremony. Commander Rilen interrogated one of the rebels, and for the past few hours security has been scanning everyone in the city. They assure me we're safe for now."

This actually made sense. Vale allowed himself a sigh of relief. "So can I go now?"

"No."

Vale looked at his brother's cold expression and tried to see into his mind. But he couldn't.

He's blocking me, thought Vale. It's like Guown said...

"I've been in meetings with my advisors all week." Cruelthor started pacing outside the prison cell. "Several of them brought to my attention the danger you represent to my rule. I have nothing against you, brother, but this is just the nature of things."

"What are you talking about? You think I'd challenge your rule?"

Oh, no, he thought fleetingly. *Am* I to be the man in the iron mask?

"Vidar, I'm your brother," he tried.

Cruelthor winced at the name. "You always were like our mother." He stopped pacing and looked at Vale, almost sadly. "And that's exactly what dad was afraid of. That's what I'm afraid of, truth be told. I can't risk having you around. I think you've figured out by now that you can't get in here-" He tapped his forehead with a smirk "-but there's still plenty of trouble you could stir up. And I can't let anything disrupt my plans. I just made several big announcements at my coronation, and people expect me to deliver. I can't constantly be watching my back, so you have to go."

Vale swallowed. "Go?"

Cruelthor rolled his eyes. “No, I’m not going to slay you. You’re to be exiled from the Northern Continent. After today, if you ever set foot on this continent again, your punishment will be swift and final.”

Shocked, Vale felt his heart racing. “But why? Cruelthor, this isn’t fair! Where am I supposed to go? I’m not going to turn on-”

“It’s done.” Cruelthor smoothed out the sleeves of his jacket.

How did this happen? thought Vale. How did everything fall apart so fast? Was that girl right – have I been blind this whole time? If I’d listened to Guown...

“But,” Cruelthor added, “lest you ever get any ideas, I’m first going to make sure people never mistake you for me.” He smirked and took a step back from the cell.

Three soldiers arrived and deactivated the force field. Vale uselessly retreated farther into the cell, but the soldiers grabbed him by the arms and dragged him out. They pulled him up the hall, and Vale looked back at his brother, who turned and walked away casually toward the far exit.

“Cruelthor! Cruelthor, you can’t do this! You’re my brother!” Panic had him now, and Vale fought not to cry as he struggled against the soldiers.

“Goodbye, good twin,” Cruelthor called back.

Vale fought against his guards, but they pulled him through the door and into a dark room.

4

Madrid

'ale stepped out of the international airport for the first time without Dominion escort. However, Cruelthor's global proclamation about 'ale's exile let everyone know he was coming, and crowds of shouting uro citizens had gathered. They mostly stood on the far side of the :curity fence that lined the airport entrance. A few drone soldiers were osted for security along the fence, but Vale knew they'd do nothing to rotect him.

They're just the standard security of the airport, he thought. If given rders, *they* would kill me. I'm on my own... Will a taxi even be willing to .ke me to a hotel? Will a hotel even admit me?

Other new arrivals exiting the airport glanced at Vale and gave him wide berth. He heard the sounds of departing planes and jets in the air :hind him, but it did nothing to dull the roar of the crowd.

"Traitor!" some yelled.

"Get the bastard!"

Some from the other persuasion shouted, "Never trust an Olander!"

I'm dead, he thought as he tried to decide which way to run. ruelthor could change his mind at any time and order me slain. ominion loyalists will try to kill me because they think I'm a traitor. :bels have already tried to kill me! I'm...

He held his lone bag against his shoulder and started to panic. Even .e air brushing against his freshly shaved scalp made him uneasy, and : reached up to touch his head only to accidentally bump the raw skin ' his brother's final gift – a Dominion sign tattoo on his left temple. ımping this with his hand also brought fresh pain from his bandaged hand where the soldiers had removed his ID tag. All this pain wa enough to distract him from keeping up his usual shield.

Immediately he was hit with sensations from the crowd. *Anger. Fea Hatred. Sadness.*

Someone threw an empty bottle. Vale ducked just in time. It hit th glass door behind him.

"Hey!" A man who'd just emerged from the door looked aroun angrily. Then he spotted Vale. The man dropped his luggage and grabbe Vale by the back of his coat. "You filthy little brat! I oughtta ring you neck! Do the world a favor!"

The crowd cheered the man on.

Vale summoned every bit of courage he had left and tried to thin He knew he had better training than the man. The man had left himse exposed, holding Vale with one arm while waving to the crowd wit other. Quickly, Vale punched the man in the gut. The man grunted an let go of Vale to steady himself.

Without another thought, Vale took off running along the road o of the airport. Those along the fence on the far side shouted and calle after him, some giving chase along the fence. Vale's legs were flying b the time the road met the main street, but he held onto his bag ar continued running, pushing his way through a group of people on th sidewalk. Crowds filled the streets here, and Vale was sure they'd stc him, but he ran on and on through the middle of the street, avoidi vehicles secured to the track system. A few angry civilians continued chase him around the traffic, but most stuck to the clogged sidewalks.

After a few blocks, Vale saw that he'd lost the mob from the airpo and now only the usual city life surrounded him.

Madrid is a huge city, he thought. If I can get out of the street, might have a chance of disappearing in the crowds.

He veered onto a sidewalk and stepped into a crowd. These peop were staring up at a screen with a sports game. The crowd was so invest in the game that they didn't notice him, and the shouts and cheers we so loud no one noticed him fighting to catch his breath. Since shaved heads were the fashion statement of the times, he hoped he could blend in.

But then the man next to him turned to high-five him. Their eyes met. The man took a step back and opened his mouth to shout.

Vale didn't wait, and he pushed back through the crowd and took off running again.

"That was Beathabane! Holy-"

A new mob started shouting behind Vale, and he ran through the streets. More and more heads turned to see what all the commotion was about, and these bystanders pointed and shouted encouragement to his pursuers. Vale rounded a street corner and looked back to see about ten large locals hot on his tail, and he hurried to cross this new street and found himself in the busiest part of downtown. Here, tall skyscrapers lined streets running in every direction. He was lost.

"He went this way!" a loud male voice shouted.

Vale looked across the street and saw a dark-skinned youth about his age. The young man was pointing down a side street that ran in the opposite direction. Vale quickly knelt behind a parked car and watched as a trio of angry pursuers turned and followed the young man as he guided them away.

"He's over here!" another male voice boomed from the far street corner.

Vale watched as this blond teen waved for the attention of other pursuers, and they followed this young man in another wrong direction.

What? Vale thought as he remained crouched behind the parked car.

"Beathabane," a female voice whispered.

Vale spun around and saw a young woman with curly, dark hair. She wore stylish civilian clothes fit for a party girl, and she had a stud diamond in her nose. She leaned casually against the building behind him and sucked on a straw that ran down into a fluorescent blue drink. She stopped drinking to smile at Vale.

He looked in her mind and heard, *"He looks so freaked out. Poor Little Lord Fauntleroy."*

He gasped. "Do you know Noctur-"

She put a finger to her lips, then motioned for him to follow her. She turned and walked to the corner of the building, then disappeared into the narrow alley.

Vale hesitated a moment, but what choice did he have? He took one more look around for danger, then darted across the sidewalk to the alley. The girl was waiting for him, and she smiled again before leading him farther down the narrow alley. Vale tried not to scrape his arms against the buildings, the space was so narrow. Eventually the girl reached a door, and she opened it and stood aside to let him enter.

Once inside, Vale's eyes adjusted to the faint light. This light came through the only window at the front of the building, and the open room appeared to be some kind of workshop. Shelves of wood stood right in front of him, benches and work stations dotted the middle of the room, and then a storefront was up by the window. It smelled of wood and dust. And metal.

The door slammed shut behind him, and Vale jumped. He turned and saw the girl grimace from the sound, but she appeared unconcerned and sucked on her drink before walking ahead of him to sit on a bench.

"Who are you and why did you bring me here?"

She smiled. "I'm Tat. No worries. We're here to rescue you."

"Who-"

The door opened again, and Vale spun to see Guown enter with Nocturna. A dark-skinned guy and a blond guy entered next, and this last arrival closed the door and locked it. Then the whole group moved to stand around him.

Vale felt uncomfortable, but he faced his old teacher. "Guown? What-"

"Good to see you're okay." Guown reached gently for Vale's head and tilted it to look at the tattoo. He made a face. "Ouch. That sore?"

"Yeah." Vale sighed. He felt like crying. He'd felt like crying all day. "Thank you for coming after me. And thank you." He looked at the two guys, knowing now they'd purposefully led the angry locals off his trail.

The dark-skinned teen shook Vale's hand. "It was a pleasure. Lost 'em three streets over. Name's Evant, by the way." His voice carried a pleasant Euro accent.

Vale smiled, liking Evant immediately.

He's not staring, thought Vale. When was the last time I met anyone who didn't stare?

The other guy, however, didn't look pleased. "I'm Dynk," was all he said. Up close, he was tall and muscular with cropped, blond hair and kind of an ugly face.

"Thank you," Vale said again.

"We don't have all day," said Nocturna to Guown.

The big man nodded and faced Vale. "I know your life's turned upside-down, lad, but come with me and we might find a way to make it all worth it. Your brother has to be stopped. I respect you for trying your way, but you know now it'll never work. If you still want to change the world, now you'll have to do it from outside the Dominion. Come with us."

Dynk muttered something.

Vale looked around at the group but didn't let himself inspect their thoughts. He was quite sure most of them didn't like him. Dynk was obvious. Evant he wasn't sure. Nocturna still looked like she thought he was a spoiled idiot. Tat seemed nice, but...

"Beathabane?" Guown squeezed his shoulder. "We have to go, lad. I'm sorry, but decide now if-"

"Okay. I'll come with you." The words were out before Vale realized he'd made up his mind. But he felt right about it immediately.

Guown slapped Vale on the arm. "Good. Good." He looked at Evant. "Let's get to the truck. Babbitt?"

They all grew silent, and Vale was about to ask what was up when Guown touched his ear and said, "Copy. We'll be there in five."

The whole group took this cue and returned to the door.

Vale nervously stepped beside Nocturna. "Babbitt?"

"He's our tech expert. He's monitoring Dominion movements from our truck." She forced a smile. "Hi, by the way."

Dynk rolled his eyes. "Flirt with the tyrant twin later, Nocturna. Let's go." He pushed past them to the door.

Nocturna's eyes narrowed at the back of Dynk's head, but she didn't say anything and followed after her group, Vale in tow.

What am I getting myself into? he thought.

A few hours later, he walked with Guown on a tour of their hideout. They were in a suburb of Madrid, for Guown explained that most rebels had to stay close to the metropolises in order to stay within range of supplies. Their hideout was in the sublevel of a luxury vehicle dealership, the owner of which had rebel sympathies.

"We divided the basement so there's a private section for the girls," Guown was saying as he walked down the hall made of scrap metal. He tapped a sliding door, which was painted pink to make things clear.

Vale looked across the wide, makeshift hall and saw a blue door of matching scrap metal on the other side. "Boys' quarters?" he asked.

"Yes." Guown's deep voice echoed off the metal, and his boots tapped on the concrete floor.

The sublevel was basically a big, empty basement divided into sections by salvaged junk.

But it is big, thought Vale. It's impressive what they've managed to cobble together. ...And it's admirable how many kids they've saved.

He'd learned that Guown's former partner – dead now – had gathered about twenty ex-Dominion Youth and hidden them here. Some, like Tat, had pure genes and so had been kicked out of the Youth rogram when their instructors found them lacking any mutate-genetic bilities. Some, like Evant, had defected during their final stages of aining because they'd refused to advance in the Dominion system. thers, like Nocturna, had been rescued when they'd wanted out but ouldn't escape otherwise. Dynk had been badly injured during an ssignment and left for dead in the field. That had changed his loyalties mewhat.

"And here's what little tech we've acquired," said Guown.

They entered a kind of cubicle room made of standing shelves and rapped wires. Electronic devices Vale didn't recognize covered the elves, and various lights and beeping sounds drew his attention this ay and that. On the far wall hung ten screens with video surveillance or ewsfeeds shining light into the room.

Babbitt, whom Vale had met earlier, turned from his seat under the reens. He removed his gigantic goggles – the use for which Vale had yet hear – and blinked at Guown. "Oh, hey. Nothing new to report, boss."

Guown grunted acknowledgement and told Vale, "We've been onitoring leads from Dominion informants. I know this is hard to ear, but your brother really is planning to make the Dominion a worse ranny than ever before. We're working on ways to stop him."

Vale read one of the rebel's hacked newsfeeds. "New Dominion RK lab to open in Berlin."

Oh, Cruelthor, he thought. What are you doing?

He looked at Guown. "What do you think I can do? I thought you anted me to overthrow my brother, but that's not going to happen ow." He pointed at his itching tattoo.

"That was more Nocturna's idea. But now, I think you can help us in her ways."

"Like what?"

Guown looked back at him with a sympathetic frown. "We'll talk out that later. You need rest. And I'm guessing something to eat?"

Exhausted, Vale nodded. Then one of the videos onscreen caught h eye. It was surveillance of Copenhagen. In fact, it showed the exterior c the very mansion Vale had grown up in.

"What-"

"Shit." Guown stepped to deactivate that screen. He looked back Vale. "You weren't supposed to see that."

"Why are you watching our old house?" Then he saw a flash c Guown's mind. "You think my mom and sister might go there?"

Guown held up a hand. "Don't get too excited. There hasn't been ar sign of them. I just thought it might be a good idea to keep an eye out fc them. I know it's important to you."

"Hell, yes, it's important!" Vale yelled in tired frustration. "W should go there now and-"

"It's too dangerous, lad. I can't let you go off and-"

"Let me? *Let* me?" Vale demanded. He felt his pulse quicken. "Am your prisoner now?"

"No, I never meant-"

"Or am I your prize now? Is that it? You want to show me off people join your rebel group?"

Guown paused and wiped his face with a hand. "You're tired. Yc have every right to be punchy. We'll talk in the morning. Just promise n you'll get some rest and not do anything stupid until we talk, okay?"

Vale crossed his arms and tried to make himself calm down.

I'm freaking out and acting like a brat, he thought. I've lo everything. I'm... I'm so tired.

He nodded at Guown and turned to walk back to the boys' sectic of the hideout.

I have nothing, he thought. I'm exiled. Branded. Forced to live hiding with rebels. Maybe I can find a way to do some good in this worl but... But my mother and little sister are out there somewhere. They're I have left, really. And if Mom is hiding from the Dominion even nc that Dad's dead, that must mean she knows the truth about Cruelth

We can't let Cruelthor get my sister – she needs to be free so she can grow up *good*, knowing the truth about everything. If I can find Mom...

He crossed paths with a rebel teen and looked down to avoid the usual stare.

Okay, the world is a mess, he thought. I might be able to work with Guown to make some things right. But I have to find my family first.

Making up his mind, Vale turned into the boys' quarters for some quick sleep.

5

Copenhagen

The train slid into the station, and Vale adjusted his coat's hood to better shadow his face. The passengers around him jostled as they pressed to the opening doors, and Vale kept his head down as he joined in the mass exodus.

The smells of the city met him first – wet pavement, cold pedestrians, the fish market up the street, and the faint bite of salty sea. He breathed in with a smile and walked with the crowd out the gate of the train station.

This was as close to a sense of *home* as he'd felt in a long time.

Exhaled clouds shot out from his mouth like dragon's breath as he jogged and watched the cobblestones of his path. He didn't dare make eye contact with anyone, and he avoided the shopping district in favor of the less populated sidewalk that ran to the shoreline. His eyes ached to look around his childhood home, but he continued with his head down. The sidewalk led into the residential district, and soon it reached the shore and ran along the concrete seawall.

Finally, Vale stopped and looked inland. There stood an open, snow-dusted park, flanked on either side by rows of tightly packed houses.

His hood secure, he dared now to look around. The houses in this neighborhood displayed beautiful feats of architecture. The sidewalk Vale had taken from the train station stretched back up into town, and everything there looked much like he remembered. Trimmed trees marked off every twenty meters of sidewalk. Light snow covered the tops of the densely packed shops. Pedestrians strolled casually, and some climbed into luxury vehicles parked on the rail system running through the streets. On the far side of the city, skyscrapers rose with glass windows that sparkled sunlight back onto the smaller buildings below. The Dominion MediTech building was the most impressive of all.

Vale knew his history. Copenhagen had once held the world's leading medical research companies. When the Euro Civil War had erupted in the wake of the DRK outbreak, many nations' top scientists had fled here to work on a cure. War and infection had struck even here, but the original Olander had found the DRK treatment in these very MediTech facilities. Copenhagen had, therefore, become the sole hope for the rest of the planet. Nations had flooded the city with whatever resources the original Olander required, and Copenhagen then became the first city restored from the war's devastation. The Dominion leaders had, therefore, always held a soft spot for Copenhagen, and it was their trophy on the Mainland-Euro.

The Dominion likes trophies, thought Vale. Was that what my mother was to my father? He brought her here from the Kota clan in the north. She was like the lovely princess of some fairy tale – at least that's how I always saw her. I think that's what Dad expected her to be too. ...I can't really blame her for leaving him.

Continuing down the sidewalk, Vale knew with every step he took that this was a bad idea. But he couldn't help it.

If I couldn't find Mom on the Continent, he thought, maybe that's because she came here. I just need to find *some* clue.

As he rounded a bend, the Dominion mansion came into view. This too, looked as it had in his childhood. He'd been born here. He'd first had Guown as a teacher here. He'd spent happy days with his mother, brother, and even his father here. It wasn't until they'd left Copenhagen that everything fell apart.

As he neared the impressive, sprawling building of stone and glass however, Vale sensed *danger*. A moment later, a Dominion patrol vehicle swung up the street and sped straight toward him. An alarm went off from the security gate of the mansion itself, and a soldier stepped from ıe security station and started running at him too. Then three more ›ldiers burst through the main doors of the mansion.

Vale turned and ran. He sped up a side street but heard the patrol ehicle following. The cold air burned his throat as he ran on and on ırough the snowy streets. He knew these streets well, but...

I have nowhere to go, he realized.

Crossing into the shopping district, he nearly ran into a woman ırrying groceries. He didn't wait to see her shocked face before he ›rinted down the sidewalk. There were too many people, however. All ‹es that met his widened in recognition, and a few people started ıouting and pointing. He crossed the street in front of a speeding luxury ʼuiser, and the sensors detected him just in time to slam the brakes. He .anced inside to see the surprise of the passengers, but he slid around the ʼuiser and hopped onto the far sidewalk to continue his flight.

A man here cut him off and shoved Vale against a parked car. "Hey!" ıe man yelled, presumably to catch the attention of any patrols nearby. 3eathabane is right here! He's right here!"

Before the man could react, Vale's adrenaline gave him the strength push the man away. The man lost his balance and fell into an outdoor .fé chair, and Vale turned to continue his run up the street.

"Stop right there!" a mechanical patrol machine ordered from ›mewhere behind.

Shit, thought Vale. Those things are fast and can fly! It'll track me ıd alert more soldiers of my location!

He looked back in his run and saw the flying machine speeding after m over the excited crowds on the sideway.

Wait, he realized as he looked down at his bandaged hand. Scanners n't detect me now that they cut the ID tag out. Ha – I don't have access my accounts, fine! At least I'm not trackable! If I can get out of this ing's sights...

Suddenly, before he could formulate a plan, an arm reached out from doorway, grabbed the front of his coat, and yanked him inside. The momentum shift nearly made him slam into the door, but he was pulle into the building and steadied on his feet. The door closed, and the ma in the shadows let him go. Then someone activated a light stick.

Vale squinted against the sudden burst of light. He stood in som kind of clothing store. Curtains were pulled over the windows. The gree glow of the light stick illuminated a group dressed in civilian clothes, bu Vale sensed their thoughts and recognized them immediately.

"Boy, what were you thinking?" Guown barked at him. He loosene a scarf around his neck before taking off gloves and slapping them dow on a table of shirts. "Of all the places to hide, you picked your ol house?"

Vale knew it had been stupid. He didn't appreciate being made to fe a fool in front of so many peers staring at him, though.

Nocturna frowned at Vale but looked up at Guown. "Go easy o him. We never would've found him if he *didn't* come here."

Guown was having none of it. "I taught you brats myself – did yo learn nothing? I swear..."

"Thank the gods he's okay," Guown was thinking. *"I'd hug the la but..."*

Dynk was positioned beside a curtained window, peeking out. "Sh incoming!"

Before any of them could move, gunfire shot out the glass windo Everyone ducked for cover. Tat screamed, and Dynk fired back with weapon he'd pulled from his coat. Nocturna crouched with Vale behi a shelf of pants, and cloth flew through the air as shots sprayed into t store.

"Head for the back exit!" Evant was yelling from behind the somewhere.

More gunshots echoed around the store as Guown and Dy continued to fire from positions on either side of the room. Then t door exploded inward as soldiers broke it down with some weapon V couldn't see. Guown fired back, and a drone soldier fell dead in the doorway, clogging it momentarily from others behind.

"Noc, get him out of here!" Guown knelt behind an upturned table and fired at the soldiers taking cover around the exterior of the doorway.

Nocturna grabbed Vale by the arm and pulled him to crouch-walk back farther into the store. "Keep down!" she yelled.

Vale hurried after her and looked back to see Dynk and Guown firing and standing to run toward the same back exit.

"We have to get to-" Guown was cut off as a spray of bullets tore apart the table beside him.

Vale watched like it was happening in slow motion. The shots' trajectory cut across Guown's path and finally caught the big man as he ran. Guown's whole body lurched to the side, and sprays of blood shot from his chest. He slumped into a shelf and looked right at Vale. Then one last bullet connected with his chest.

"No!" Vale screamed.

But they'd reached the back exit, and Nocturna pulled him to the door just as Dynk slid across the floor to avoid more gunfire. Together they scrambled out the door into an alleyway. Vale tried to wrestle off Nocturna and run back inside, and that's when Dynk hit him in the head with the butt of his gun.

Everything went black, and Vale slumped into Dynk's arms.

6

Melonia

When he woke, he didn't even ask if Guown was dead. The tears in her eyes and the tears on her cheeks told him.

"Where are we now?" he asked instead. He sat up on the cot and looked around.

The bedroom was old, but functional. Nocturna sat on a chair by his cot. Partially open blinds clacked against the window frame as a breeze blew in from the night.

"Does it matter?" she finally answered with a sigh.

He watched as she wiped her face with the back of her sleeve. She looked tired and sad, which he'd expected.

"It's my fault."

"Yes."

He winced. He'd expected her to be a little gentler.

But that's not the world we live in, he thought. No time for gentle. I shouldn't expect to be coddled anymore. Especially not now. Not after...

"He's dead because of me," he said to drive the point home to himself.

Nocturna looked at him without emotion. "Yes, but he wasn't a man destined to die in his sleep. And when he woke us in the middle of the night to go after you, he told us he believed you're worth risking our lives for. Are you, Little Lord?"

Knowing the weight of this guilt would probably never leave him, Vale could only shrug. "I don't know. I was so desperate and selfish that I..."

"You wanted to find your mom and sister. I wouldn't call that selfish exactly."

"But it was still stupid and pointless. They weren't there. And Guown..." Vale pinched back tears. "I don't know why he thought I'm worth it, Nocturna. I really don't."

"He's kind of a mess," Nocturna was thinking. *"I guess that's better than thinking he deserves to be king of the Mainland. That's what Dynk thinks he wants."*

Vale swallowed and let his eyes wander around the room to avoid both their thoughts. He hated that he was about to beg, but... "I'd like to stay, if you think the group would let me. I certainly don't deserve to stay. But I have nowhere else to go."

She lifted her eyes to his. Not finding whatever she wanted there, she let out a short chuckle and swept a hand over her braided mohawk. "You don't get it, do you? It's not a matter of us *letting* you stay. We need you. You just need to pull your shit together. I know I've given you a lot of crap, but I *do* believe you're worth the trouble. Guown always said he saw something in you. Something great. And... Well, Guown wanted me to support you, so I will. I think I understand now what Guown really wanted." She raised an eyebrow. "You're meant to lead us, Little Lord."

Vale sat back on the cot in surprise and shook his head. "The others would never let me-"

"We're starting a movement here," she countered. "The others know that. What better way to get the world's attention than to be a rebel force led by the rebel twin brother of our enemy?"

"I can't lead you. Nocturna, I almost got all of you killed. I *did* get Guown killed!" He rubbed his face with his hands.

Nocturna reached and took his hands from his face so he had to look at her. "I know you're new to this way of life, but... Things happen. We don't live in a world where we're allowed the luxury of dwelling on how things could've gone differently. If we want to accomplish anything, we quickly mourn our dead and push ahead as best we can. I think our best way is with you leading us."

"But no one trusts me!" he said in frustration. "Your own people ok at me and see Cruelthor. I can't go anywhere without everyone nowing who I am." He pointed at the tattoo.

"But don't you see? That's exactly it – you can show the world who ou really are." She looked at him with *sympathy*. "Guown knew you ave a good heart. He knew you have Olander greatness without all the lander evil. He wanted you to join us because he knew – even when ou were blind to your brother's true nature – that you *want* to be a etter person than your brother. You never agreed with the Dominion hilosophy, and Guown knew that. He knew you wanted to change erything. Leading us gives you that opportunity."

Vale looked at the floor. Was she right? Was this his chance? This *uld* be his way to fix everything the Dominion had ruined. He could and for everything he'd always wanted the Dominion to stand for. orking with Guown's chosen pupils, he could fight back and change ings.

Guown believed in me, he thought with a heavy heart. He saved my e at least three times. I owe him this.

Nocturna seemed to sense he was changing his mind. "Come on." e patted his knee and stood, then waited for him to stand.

When he did, he took a deep breath and followed her to the door. creaked open, and together they walked into a hall. Ahead the hall ened into a living room. It looked like a cheap apartment. Three ismatched couches lined the living room, and crates were propped up r tables. Evant, Dynk, and Babbitt lounged on the couches while Tat t cross-legged on the floor. Each had an open can and fork. All stopped ting and looked up as Nocturna and Vale entered the room.

"About time you woke up," muttered Dynk. He forked a chunk of eat and shoved it into his mouth.

"We need to make some decisions," Nocturna told the group.

Tat set aside her finished meal. "Always straight to the point, Noc."

"Then let's get to it," said Dynk. "What are we going to do about th Tyrant Twin?" He glared at Vale.

"Dynk, cool it." Evant set his can on the arm of his couch. He looke at Vale. "No one here blames you for Guown's death – we all loved th old bastard, but he knew the risks of going after you and accepted then We all did. And Guown would've done the same thing for any one of u We're family – we look after our own." He looked at the others, with tone. "Anyone here disagree with that?"

Some of the others exchanged glances, but no one spoke up.

Vale looked around the room. "If anyone here doesn't want me t join this group, I'll go."

Babbitt adjusted his goggles. "Guown vouched for you. That's goc enough for me."

Tat smiled and gave Vale a thumbs up.

Dynk seemed to waver, but he rolled his eyes and nodded.

Vale felt more relief than he'd expected. "I know my being he puts you in extra danger. Believe me, I'm aware of that." He thought Guown falling to the floor. Quickly he blinked the image away and face Nocturna. "But you were right in Vancouver. Because I was a Dominic heir, I can do more damage than the rest of you."

She raised an eyebrow.

Tat, looking between them from her spot on the floor, raised h hand. "What are you talking about?"

Evant drummed his fingers on his biceps in thought. "Beathaba knows things. Not just Dominion education – we all have that – but knows Dominion secrets that were above our paygrade. He knows ba locations. Drone movements. DRK treatment transport routes."

Vale nodded.

Even Dynk realized this gave them an advantage. "So we could atta the Dominion where it hurts. We'd be able to do even more damage th the Underground."

"And maybe," said Tat, "we could flush away Cruelthor's glorious plans for that factor base here on the Mainland."

Nocturna nodded. "I think this is what Guown wanted. And..." She glanced at Evant. "With Guown gone, I think we should put Beathabane in charge."

Everyone had some reaction to this. *Shock* was the overwhelming feeling that hit Vale. And *anger. Confusion.*

Dynk scoffed. "Are you kidding me? He lost his other kingdom, so you're just going to hand him ours? We can't trust an Olander!"

Nocturna argued as she had with Vale. "Having Beathabane as the face of our movement will make everyone pay attention and-"

"And hate us!" argued Dynk.

Tat tried to calm them down. "With Guown gone, we do need a new-"

"He got Guown killed!"

"Enough!" Evant stood from the couch and walked to Vale's side. "Guown brought him here for this reason. This exact reason. He told me so before we went to Vancouver. Guown wanted Beathabane to lead our entire rebel group, and he selected each of us to be in his top team. That's why we've been training together – it's all for him."

That shocked everyone into silence, even Vale.

"I never wanted command," Evant went on. "Guown was only grooming me for it in case Plan A didn't work." He pointed a thumb back at Vale. "I've always thought this is a good idea. Beathabane knows how we can hurt the Dominion. It'll be a risk to follow him, sure, but what *isn't* a risk? We're rebels. We can't go home. We can't have normal lives." He looked at Tat, then Dynk. "We can make the Dominion regret throwing us away. We can make them regret thinking we don't matter."

Everyone paused in thought. The air was thick with emotions, and Vale had to shut them out. He tried to sort out his own state. The first thing he noticed was that his palms were sweating.

Evant looked at Vale. "But I'm leaving it up to you. Do you want to lead us? I know it was all Guown's crazy idea and you had no idea, but...here we are."

Vale looked at the others, all facing him now. He swallowed.

I've always wanted to make the world better, he thought. Now I just have to do it from the outside. Against my brother.

"I'll always have Olander blood, you're right." He nodded at Dynk. "But you can trust me. I swear it. The Dominion was never my home. I thought I could make it something better than what it was, but that's never going to happen. But as a rebel, as one of you, I intend to show the world a better way. I just need your help to do it."

That's all I've got in the way of grand speeches, he thought nervously.

Evant addressed the group. "We have to be together on this before we go back to the others at the hideout. So let's vote. All in favor of Beathabane becoming our leader, raise your hand." He lifted his own arm.

Tat immediately threw hers in the air. As did Nocturna. Dynk and Babbitt looked at each other, then Babbitt shrugged and raised his hand.

Dynk let out a huff. "Well, I can tell you one thing – I'm not following anyone who wears a Dominion sign tattoo. Follow me, Tyrant Twin." He stood from the couch and walked to the exit, then waited to see if Vale would follow.

Vale looked to Evant for help.

Evant smirked, put a hand on Vale's shoulder, and walked to the door. "Come on. I think I know what he has in mind."

7

Berlin

One year later

Dynk smacked the executive across the face. The man tilted in his chair, but Tat had bound him tightly. Evant held the chair steady from behind with a foot pressed against one of its legs.

"Where is your rendezvous to pay the operative?" Dynk asked again.

The executive's lavish hotel suite was the nicest they'd been in for some time, so no one was in a terrible rush to escape back to the streets of Berlin. A Dominion-secured city, Berlin certainly wasn't the safest location for a mission. Fortunately, Babbitt had done a thorough security wipe-down of the hotel, so no monitors would be alerted to their presence any time soon.

They were, however, in a hurry to discover the location of the executive's rendezvous. Sometime tonight, he was supposed to hand over a briefcase full of kronar to a Dominion operative awaiting payment for a job well done. This job had involved releasing a canister of DRK into a nearby village where Underground rebels were hiding. Thereafter, Cruelthor had ordered the executive to pay the operative and assign him his next target. Babbitt had luckily intercepted Cruelthor's transmission when scanning for anything that might give them a lead on Dominion activity in the area.

The Underground commanders are mostly assholes, thought Vale, but they're doing a lot of good in this region. We can't let them be wiped out. Besides, Cruelthor shouldn't get away with factoring an entire village.

Tat was rummaging in the mini-fridge. "Oh, yes! Guys, he has chocolate!" Her dark curls bounced as she popped up from the fridge.

Smiling, she held two handfuls of expensive chocolate bars. She threw one across the kitchenette's marble counter to Nocturna, and then Tat tore open her own and started dancing around, making sounds of pleasure as she chewed.

Nocturna made a 'why not?' face and opened her chocolate, took a bite, and winked at Vale.

Vale wore a coat with a wide hood to shadow his face, but he shook his head at her with a smirk. Then he indicated the open briefcase on the counter in front of her. "How much?"

"Looks like over a million." Nocturna trailed her hand over rows and rows of loose kronar tubes, their fiberoptics lit in different hues to indicate their varying denominations. "I've never seen this much kronar at once. I almost want to lick them."

Vale turned his attention to where Babbitt sat at the executive's desk. "Any progress?"

Babbitt's fingers were flying over the desktop controls, and file after file opened and closed on the holographic screen over the tech-laced wallpaper. "He's wiped his files pretty clean. He didn't use his own account to extract that much loose kronar, but I can't find the ID account he did use. I'm getting a lot of financial records from his palm scans, though. We might be able to track his movements and figure out where he's been lately, so that *might* lead us to his rendezvous if he scoped it out earlier, but..."

Nocturna walked over to Vale. "Sir, you know the quickest way to get the truth."

Vale sighed and turned to where Dynk was interrogating the executive.

Most of the time, they managed to carry out their missions without having to expose who he was. In some instances, however, his telepathy was required. He didn't like revealing his cards too often, however, especially when they planned to let the interrogated party walk away.

Vale put a hand on Dynk's shoulder, and his friend turned his blond ead to frown at Vale.

"Are you sure?" Dynk thought at him. *"If he figures out what you're oing, he'll tell everyone he knows that you're telepathic. I thought you idn't want-"*

"We don't have time any other way," Vale said aloud.

Evant looked at Vale pointedly, and Vale used their mind link to hear is thoughts.

"Try talking it out of him," thought Evant. *"He's not one to crack from rce – that's clear. But coercion might work. He's too slippery to risk letting im know you're telepathic. We'd have to kill him if he figured it out."*

Vale nodded at Evant. Dynk stepped aside, and now Vale looked own at the captive executive. The man clearly didn't recognize Vale t because of the hood shadowing his face, but with dramatic flair ale reached up and removed the hood from his shaved head. Vale saw cognition in the man's widened eyes, then his eyes darted to the side of ale's head to quickly check for the Dominion tattoo.

Even after all this time, thought Vale, people still momentarily think m Cruelthor.

In annoyed amusement, Vale rolled his eyes and reached up to touch e slash mark that Dynk had once tattooed over the Dominion sign. 'es, it's me," he told the executive. "The other one."

The executive swallowed. He was sweating, and his bottom lip was eeding from Dynk's work. "I won't tell you rebels anything. If ruelthor ever finds out I talked to *you*-"

"Whatever comes next you can blame on the operative," Vale said lmly. "*He* isn't going to report anything to Cruelthor ever again. If u carry on as normal after this, my brother will never know you had ything to do with this. My friend at your computer has blocked your) tag activity since we grabbed you, and all monitor surveillance has en looped for this hotel. As far as anyone knows, you're just taking a p right now before going to pay the operative. We were never here. If you tell me what I want to know, you'll walk away with half the krona you were planning to give the operative."

That got the man's attention. He glanced at Dynk nearby. "How do know you won't just slay me?"

"I guess trust needs to run both ways. You tell me the truth abo where I can find the operative, and I'll let you live with even more wealt than you currently possess." He gave the man a moment to consider, the looked him in the eye and pushed into his mind *greed* and *fear*. "If yo don't tell me where to find the operative, Dynk will make sure you nev taste chocolate again. Or anything else."

Dynk pulled out a knife and stuck out his tongue, knowing Val point.

"I'm flushed," thought the executive. *"But I could use the kronar. Beathabane's right; I can say I paid the operative and then don't know wh happened after I sent him to the BMO factory."*

Vale tried not to show a reaction to this. The BMO factory was in a abandoned suburb that had once been a main manufacturing district. made sense that the Underground would have a base there. It made eve more sense that it would be Cruelthor's next target.

"Alright," the executive finally said. He looked across the room at th clock. "I'm supposed to meet the operative at the Oberbaum Bridge ten minutes."

Vale focused on the man's mind and sensed *sincerity, hope, reli* Then he nodded at Evant.

"Thank you," Evant told the man with a kick to his chair. "Dynk an Tat, stay here with him until we're back. Babbitt-"

"Yeah, yeah," Babbitt called from the computer terminal. "Keep th monitors oblivious and scrounge around for anything useful while you' away. Got it."

Nocturna, carrying the briefcase, joined Evant and Vale as th reached the hotel suite's exit. "Let's go catch us a bad guy."

About ten minutes later, Evant and Nocturna walked across the famous bridge from one direction while Vale strolled from the other. Centuries of use and war had been kind to the bridge. Dominion reconstruction had been even kinder. Vale watched his brick and concrete path as he walked, and the smell of purified city water wafted up from the river. Beautiful lampposts lit the bridge rails. Several wealthy (and therefore Dominion) pedestrians smiled and chatted as they sauntered along the bridge. Many tourists carried shopping bags, and a few ate pastries from the bakery Vale had passed on his way. His stomach rumbled, but he adjusted his grip on the briefcase and focused on his mission.

"Don't see anyone fishy yet," Evant's mind-voice called to Vale.

Neither do I, thought Vale.

He sensed a wave of *frustration* from Evant. Vale knew Evant thought they had better things to do than watch the backs of Underground rebels. Just yesterday Babbitt had uncovered a route the Dominion was using to bring prisoners to the Mainland's new factor base. Rescuing these prisoners was actually Vale's #1 priority. However, then they'd heard the news about the factored village outside Berlin. Vale couldn't let Cruelthor's heinous attack go unpunished.

Those villagers didn't deserve being factored, thought Vale. No one does. And I'm certainly not going to let it happen again to this next target.

Just then, ahead, Vale spotted a solitary man leaning against the rail of the bridge. He had checked his watch twice since within sight. He kept looking in Vale's direction as if expecting someone.

"I think that's him," said Nocturna's mind-voice.

Vale looked past the man and saw Nocturna and Evant approaching from the other direction. Adjusting his path so that he could cut off the man if he ran, Vale tugged his hood farther over his face and walked with the briefcase in clearer view. The case reflected the lights of the bridge, and the shine of light-on-metal caught the potential operative's attention. The man studied the briefcase, and his mind flushed with *greed* and *satisfaction.*

Bingo, thought Vale.

The man stepped away from the rail and examined Vale as he walked closer. "Excuse me. Do you happen to know-"

Then the light must've caught Vale at just the right angle, and the operative's face froze in horror.

Shit, thought Vale.

The operative turned to run in the opposite direction, but Nocturna and Evant were right there to meet him.

"Shh." Nocturna reached out and grabbed the man's wrist, skin to skin. "Sleep."

Her mutate-genetic ability to sedate through touch worked quickly. The operative tottered before completely going limp, and Evant caught him as he slumped. Quickly, Evant threw one of the man's arms over his shoulder to support him.

By now, pedestrians were watching.

"Oh, Andru," Nocturna scolded loudly. "Always drunk before even getting to the party."

Vale took the man's other arm to support him from that side. Together he and Evant dragged away the unconscious operative.

"Any idea where his next target was?" asked Evant.

"Yeah, I heard the executive thinking about the BMO factory. We need to find this guy's vehicle and make sure that next DRK canister never gets delivered."

Nocturna was quite pleased with herself. She skipped ahead, twirling her purse – never mind the gun inside – as she ran ahead. "I'll find Andru's car."

It was late by the time they reached the BMO factory. Vale had driven the operative's car out of downtown Berlin, through the poorer streets of the suburbs, and finally into the old manufacturing district. The entire area was in ruins from centuries of war, but it was clear that the citizens were trying to restore the town. Vale had seen many similar situations during his past year on the Mainland – anywhere there was anything salvageable, citizens were trying to rebuild, especially if it meant living close to a Dominion metropolis. It wasn't surprising the Underground had a base here, for they too needed to be close to supplies.

Vale parked the car at the rusted gate of the factory and shut off the engine. The rebel trio climbed out, and Evant lifted the unconscious operative over his shoulder. Then they stood together, in the clouded moonlight, and looked through the gate at the forsaken building. No lights. No sounds of humanity. The breeze brought smells of mold and rust.

"Sure this is right?" asked Evant.

Nocturna walked to the control panel by the gate. She flicked the buttons. "Dead."

A loud voice cut over the wind, "Dead is exactly what you'll be unless you put your hands in the air right now!"

Vale and Nocturna held up their hands and looked around. From a cluster of trees along the road, a soldier with a rifle hurried towards them. Evant turned with the operative and slowly slid the unconscious man to the ground. Then he too raised his arms.

Another soldier appeared from the trees and joined the first. "Who are you people?"

"No questions until we get them inside," said the first soldier. He waved his weapon at them and pointed to the gate. "It's open. Move. I'm taking you to Commander Scribe. Be quick, before we're spotted out here."

Evant sent Vale a look. *"They're taking us into their base? Good lord, these people are idiots! They don't know who we are, if we brought backup, if we're armed..."*

"Do as they say," Vale told his partners.

Keeping his hands over his hooded head, he waited until Nocturna opened the gate. Then he led them inside the compound. The gravel parking lot was bare, and Vale studied the factory as they approached. Windows too high to escape from. Only the one cargo door. The side door they were headed for seemed the only way to quietly get in or out.

Suddenly, this door opened, and the soldiers behind ushered them inside.

Immediately inside, light sticks illuminated the open factory floor. Dozens of Underground soldiers worked among rows of vehicles. A squad of soldiers had been alerted and hurried their way, and the man in the lead was obviously the commander in charge. He was in his early fifties, fit, with balding hair. He wore the standard Underground uniform, as did his men, but his face wore as serious an expression as Vale had ever seen, and his eyes held all the signs of authority.

This must be Commander Scribe, thought Vale. I hope this was a good idea...

"Bring them to my office," Scribe ordered the soldiers guarding them. He stepped through a door into a side room, which in the factory's former life had been a processing office.

Once ushered inside this office, Vale watched as their soldier escorts lowered the operative into a chair. The man was still out cold from Nocturna's gift. Scribe paid the unconscious man no mind but leaned on his desk and listened as the soldiers quickly explained what had happened.

Evant was staring at the ceiling, trying to keep quiet about the stupidity of these soldiers' tactics.

Nocturna looked at Vale and shrugged.

They hadn't even handcuffed Vale. Quickly, he reached up and pushed the hood off his face.

The soldiers whipped around because of his sudden movement, and they shouted an alarm when they saw his face. Weapons rose to aim at all three newcomers, and Vale momentarily regretted his action.

"Hold," Scribe ordered his men. He looked at Vale for a solid minute, ien paid Evant and Nocturna a passing glance.

I might regret this, thought Vale, but...

Meeting the commander's eyes, Vale sent feelings of *calm*, *trust*, and *cceptance* into Scribe's mind. Then he telepathically said, *"It's okay, sir. Ve come in peace. This man is the operative who released the DRK into the illage where some of your people were hiding. We thought it right that he e handed over to the Underground, so we brought him to you when we arned that this base was his next target."*

Once the commander's mind was returned to his own control, he umped and sat on the desk. He held up a hand to his men that he was kay, and then he looked at Vale again. "Holy shit, kid."

"Sir?" asked a soldier.

Scribe wiped his face. "Clear the room. All of you."

"Sir?"

"Do it." He glared, and his men rushed to obey.

Soon the door closed, and Vale, Nocturna, Evant, and the nconscious operative were alone in the room with the commander.

The older man gave Vale a hesitant look. "I'm not sure I can say it's a easure to meet you, Beathabane, but I'm Commander-"

"Scribe," Vale finished. He nodded. "Yes, sir. I caught that. I don't ean to be rude, but we're in a bit of a rush. I can't ever stay in public ng, and so many of your men have seen me..."

Scribe remained seated on the edge of his desk and seemed to still be ellecting himself.

"First time with a telepath, sir?" asked Nocturna with a grin.

Scribe chuckled and shook off his thoughts. "Alright, son. I can't elieve I'm going to say this, but I trust you. I take it you want mething, or else why would you hand-deliver this scum?" He glared at e sleeping operative.

"I brought him here so you could deal with him as you see fit," said ale. He shrugged. "You people deserve justice for what happened to that village, so I wanted to bring you the guy responsible. I though at the very least, that we should warn you the Dominion knows abou this base. You should get your people to safety before Cruelthor tries t factor everyone here."

"Not that the Underground would warn us if roles were reverse thought Evant.

Vale ignored this and sensed in Scribe's mind that the man was sti trying to decide what to do. The Underground wasn't known for kin treatment of Dominion defectors. Scribe seemed to be wrestling wit that now.

And the Underground tried to kill me once before, Vale thought he remembered the attack in Vancouver's woods.

"Also," Vale added hurriedly, "we have half a million kronar in briefcase in our car. Take it. I'm sure you can put it to good use."

"Beathabane," Evant said aloud in surprise.

Nocturna sighed and rubbed her forehead. "Tat's going to disappointed. She was going to buy so much jewelry with her cut."

Vale tried not to roll his eyes at his partners and instead faced Scrib

The commander had an eyebrow raised at the sum. "Okay. Than you. I imagine you want me to report this to my superiors to convin them you're a good guy? I'm sure you've heard that all bases have be ordered to refuse you if you seek asylum in our camps?"

"Yeah. I heard that." Vale shuffled on his feet. "I'd appreciate a good word you could put in for me. For us."

Scribe's gaze wandered to Evant and Nocturna. He seemed amuse "This your team? A bunch of kids?"

Evant's dark brow furrowed. "We're not *kids*. And even if we we brainwashed in the Dominion Youth, we're still better trained than h your-"

"Not helping," Nocturna said through a fake smile.

Scribe chuckled. "What do you call yourselves? Beathabane's Ba of Merry Men, or something like that?"

"We're called the Hood," Evant said with a glare.

The commander faced Vale again, his eyes moving – as everyone's did – to the tattoo. "Yeah, I'm guessing you have to cover yourself as much as possible."

Vale reached up to replace the hood over his head. He had a flash of a childhood memory when Vedanleé had done the same thing with the black cloak she'd always worn. Everyone thought he'd named his rebel group after his own hood – he alone kept the secret that he thought of his mom every time he used the disguise.

Scribe was still thinking. "Since your brother exiled you, there've been rumors about why he hates and fears you so much. I think I'm starting to see why – I assume he knows you can read his mind?"

Frowning, Vale nodded.

"Makes sense." Scribe scratched his jaw and sighed, looking at the operative. "Well, you'd better get out of here before any of my men report you're here. I'll try to talk to my superiors, but I can't promise anything."

"I understand." With that, Vale motioned for Evant and Nocturna to follow him out.

Leaving the office, Vale walked between his friends and headed for the exit. He glanced around from under his hood and saw soldiers around the factory staring now. Word had spread fast. He heard whispers, and he saw a few soldiers point at him. Quickening his pace, he lowered his head, pulled his hood lower, and watched his steps.

"Come on," said Nocturna as she opened the door. "Let's get back to the others."

It was the middle of the night when the trio finally returned to the executive's hotel suite. They entered to find Tat sleeping on the giant bed, surrounded by the loose kronar tubes they'd promised the executive. Dynk sat in a chair opposite their prisoner, who'd been cleaned up and moved onto a sofa, though his hands were still tied. Babbitt sat at the computer terminal.

"All good?" called Dynk.

"Yeah," said Evant with a glance at Vale.

Vale hadn't spoken much on their return trip.

We're all seen as untrustworthy, he thought. But Evant, Nocturna, Dynk... Their origins might be forgiven by the other rebels eventually. They might be able to prove their worth so they can fight right alongside the Underground. But my face will never be accepted. The rebels won't ever forget exactly where I come from.

Nocturna came and stood with Vale by the kitchenette's counter. She put a hand on his arm kindly, and the human contact eased his tension – although he didn't think she was using her gift.

"I'm okay," he told her with a weak smile. He pushed his hood off his head and rubbed his shaved head.

Nocturna leaned beside him against the counter. "We're with you, Vale. You know that."

"Uh, guys," Babbitt called from the computer.

Vale looked over and saw Babbitt waving for him.

With Nocturna by his side, Vale walked over as Evant also joined them. Together they stood in front of the giant screen. A newsfeed was paused, and Babbitt activated the controls once they were paying attention.

"It's a joyous day at the new Capitol," the reporter was saying. She stood with a large crowd in front of the enormous Dominion compound. "After months and months of search, Cruelthor's long-lost sister has at last been found."

Vale gasped.

"She was brought to Capital City this morning," the reporter went on. "We haven't received much news yet except that she is a healthy, seven-year-old girl and that Cruelthor is absolutely thrilled to have her home."

"Shit," said Evant.

The newsfeed switched stories, and Babbitt reached forward and deactivated the system.

Vale took a step back and leaned on the counter.

She's alive, he thought. All this time, I thought maybe Cruelthor lied to me and wanted me to find her so he could kill her. Thank God she's alright.

He turned and rested his head on the cool marble counter, tuned out the others, and cried in relief.

But where is Mom? he thought suddenly. How did Cruelthor get our sister away from her? I don't think he killed Mom – if he'd killed her, he would've bragged about it with a public announcement. Mom must still be out there somewhere. I guess there's nothing more I can do. Wherever she is, she's always managed to protect herself before. And now at least I know where my sister is. I can stop worrying...

Finally, Nocturna's hand on his back couldn't be ignored. "Beathabane?"

He stood up and faced his friends. He gave them a smile, not quite of happiness but certainly of relief. "She's alive."

Nocturna nodded with a sympathetic smile. "What do you want us to do? She's your sister. If you want, we'll go back with you. We'll find a way to the Northern Continent so we can rescue her."

Vale looked around at his team. At his family.

We'd never be able to break into the Capitol compound, he thought. I'd get them all killed – and I've certainly learned my lesson about risking their lives for my personal vendettas.

He took a deep breath. "No, we're not going to rescue her."

Nocturna made a face. "Are you sure?"

"If we somehow did manage to rescue her, Cruelthor would just keep hunting until he found her. For whatever reason, he really wants her with him. Besides, she's only a little kid – she'd never be safe living like we do. She's safer where she is, at least for now."

Nocturna accepted this. “You’re right. If we brought her to live with us, Cruelthor would probably consider her an enemy too.”

Evant agreed. “That’d put her in even more danger.”

Vale pulled his hood over his head. He smiled at Nocturna and told the group, “We’d better get out of here. Someone wake up Tat and let her take all the chocolate she can carry.”

Dominion Newsfeed

07/08/69 22:00
Paris, Crow's Region, Mainland-Euro
– ALERT: Unauthorized Streaming Video Upload
...Tracking coordinates...

he dark room is silent for a moment as Beathabane appears to be inking over the reporter's question. Kaytrine glances at the camera ervously, no doubt hoping she hasn't upset her important interviewee.

"Sir," she says for his attention. "I'm sorry if this is too personal, but a t of people are wondering. What are you going to do about your sister? /hy haven't you attempted to rescue her?"

Finally, Beathabane says, "It's the greatest regret of my life that I uldn't find my sister before Cruelthor found her. But everything I do for her. I've said that I hope to set an example that will prompt others join us in this fight. I hope to set that example for my sister also. I ave to be her good example – I have to show her a better way to live an what my brother shows her. A better alternative." He looks into the mera, and he grows more confident. "The most important thing I can o is save as many people as I can from the evils of my brother. I try to o my part, but we must all work together to fight for a better world. A orld where people are free. A world where people aren't condemned by e government to live a hell on Earth as factors. We rebels must stop ghting amongst ourselves. Those of us who've escaped the Dominion – d I pray my sister joins us someday – are not the enemy. We rebels must nite to bring down the Dominion. My brother must be stopped."

Off-camera, a male voice calls, "Sir! I see Dominion speeders pproaching from the east!"

Kaytrine reaches for her headset device like she's about to jump u and run, but Beathabane motions for her to wait. He glances to the sid and smiles at someone.

“I once read an ancient story about a man in an iron mask who wa imprisoned by an evil king. Legend has it that the man was the king twin, and the king hid him away so that he could never challenge th king.” Beathabane turns his shaved head for the camera to see the slashe Dominion tattoo. “My twin had a different approach, as you all kno But in my marked exile I've challenged his rule every way I can. Yo might not trust my face. You might not trust my ex-Dominion follower But we will never rest until the Dominion's evils are undone. Trust i that.”

Kaytrine reaches to shake his hand. “Thank you, Beathabane. I'v heard a lot about you, and you're apparently as scholarly as they say. An inspiring. I hope you don't mind if I try to find a more respectful title f you than ‘Beathabane,’ sir.”

He smiles. “That would be appreciated. I-”

“Sir!”

“Evant, can you see-”

Beathabane stops when suddenly the spotlight goes offline, and th whole room is now dark.

The same male voice, presumably Evant, calls through the darknes “My coms aren't working!”

“Mine either!” says a new female voice.

Beathabane responds calmly. “They've zapped the power out of th building.”

The cameraman speaks up. “Ha! Not the whole building! I've rigge this thing to run on a looped system that can't be-”

“We'd better get out of here,” says Evant. “They'll storm the stairwe first.”

“Nocturna,” Beathabane orders, “go check our exit.”

“Okay, I'm on it,” says the woman.

The noise of a chair scraping back is loudest over other noises of scuffling.

"Thank you," Beathabane must be saying to Kaytrine.

"Merci," she answers. She groans angrily, then continues to speak in a stream of Dominion-unauthorized babble.

"Ah, crap," says the cameraman. "The power cut must've knocked her translator offline too."

"That's exactly what she just said," says Evant.

Kaytrine tries in English, "I thank for interview. Okay if I call you... Poet Heroic? That not right. I mean..."

"No," laughs Beathabane. "That's perfect. I'd be honored."

"Sir," says Evant, "we have to go!"

Sounds of gunfire erupt from some distance away.

"Yeah, sounds like the end of an interview to me," says the cameraman.

Excerpt from The Kota (The Kota Series Book 1)

Lee's expression was one of complete confusion as he looked up from within the cryogenic bed and saw Trok kneeling beside him. Reviving him had been a shockingly easy procedure, but the Kota scientists with Trok had prepared for this their whole lives.

Lee coughed and struggled to sit up in the steaming cryo bed.

"It's alright," said Trok. "You're okay. Just take it easy."

He was so excited and relieved to see Lee alive that he nearly grabbed him in a long-overdue embrace. Instead, he placed a hand on Lee's shoulder to steady him. Trok was tense for several reasons, but first off he wanted to make sure Lee was okay.

He's my long-lost little brother, thought Trok. Please, oh, please, just let him be okay!

As the doctors examined him, Lee looked beyond Trok at the dozen men and women gathered. Then he looked around the lab-cave. Trok knew Lee would see immediately that a good deal of time had passed – the state of the lab-cave showed centuries of disuse. Trok and the descendents of the Kota remnant had always kept a careful eye on the place, but some things couldn't fight age. Faint running lights hummed overhead, but the balcony around their lower level had rusted long ago and collapsed in places. Most of the ancient machinery was broken. Only the life support functions remained intact, though the system had been repaired many times by the Kota assigned to guard over Lee throughout the years.

Lee looked back at Trok and examined his face. Lee himself had physically aged maybe ten to fifteen years while sleeping. Now middle-aged, his forehead was wrinkled. His hair and beard were peppered gray. His body underneath the medical scrubs appeared only minimally atrophic, though very pale.

"You..." Lee cleared his throat to find his voice. "You were frozen too?"

Trok lifted an eyebrow. "Not exactly. Let the doctors check you over, and then we'll take you out of here. I'll explain everything once we're safely away."

"These are the Kota?"

"Yes."

"How long has it been?"

Trok hesitated, knowing this would be hard, but there was no real way to ease into it. "Five hundred years."

Lee's eyes widened, but he'd been prepared for this. He asked no more as the doctors finished examining him.

The doctor in charge stood, lowered his x-ray scanner, and turned to Trok. "Sir, he's as stable as we could've hoped. I think we're safe to move him. He's weak and groggy, but that'll wear off soon."

"Good." Relieved by this news, Trok focused on the next concern. He lowered his voice so as not to worry Lee. "I don't want to stay here any longer than necessary. I'm sure Dominion patrols check this place on a daily basis in hopes of intercepting us."

"Good thing we brought soldiers, then."

Yes, thought Trok bleakly. Kota soldiers, anyway. And we've only got five with us. They'd be no match for Dominion drone soldiers.

"I'd rather we didn't have to use them," he told the doctor. "We can't afford getting caught in a firefight." He looked down at his brother.

The doctor nodded and turned to help his partners with their patient. Lee seemed curious about why the Kota deferred to Trok, but he allowed himself to be lifted into a wheelchair. Once he was ready, the whole group hurried for the ancient building's exit.

Outside, the warm sunlight pouring down didn't bother Trok's eyes. He looked over the wilderness beyond the crumbling gates, searching for danger. Trok saw Lee take a deep breath of fresh air and close his eyes to feel the sunshine. This once again reminded Trok how disconnected he was from everything around him.

But now Lee's with me, thought Trok. I'm not as alone anymore. I just hope he can handle this.

"No patrol activity in the area, sir," called a Kota soldier from his position near a hover hummer.

Trok snapped into action and took over wheeling his brother toward his soldier's vehicle. "Let's be sure we're gone before they arrive."

"Yes, sir." The soldier whistled to his partners. "Load up!"

The Kota doctors and soldiers piled into the other vehicles as Trok helped Lee into the backseat of their hover hummer. Once Lee was secure, Trok closed his door and stepped around the vehicle to climb in the other side. He watched as the first hummer started off toward the road.

So far, so good.

Inside the hummer, Trok ordered their driver to go. They took off smoothly, and Trok relaxed enough to face his brother. He remembered the last time they'd been here – at the lab-cave, in a hover vehicle, with a Kota driver.

Things are so different now, he thought.

Lee took a drink from a thermos the doctors gave him. "I don't think I can wait until we get to wherever it is you're taking me." He was coming to life a bit. "What's happened?"

See more at SunshineSomerville.com

About the Author

Sunshine Somerville has a degree in English Literature and self-published her first book at the ripe old age of nine. She currently lives on the beachy side of Michigan with her husband, daughters, and rescued dogs.

The Kota Series is a Science Fantasy epic based on youthful obsessions with X-Men, Star Wars, The Chronicles of Narnia, Dark Angel, and A Wrinkle in Time.

.

The Alt-World Chronicles is an Urban Fantasy series inspired by weird recurring dreams, a brainstorming session in the shower, and one ridiculously hot summer lived in Kansas City.

.

A Fairly Fairy Tale is Sunshine's first Middle Grade Fantasy book. She got the idea from her family's crest, which portrays a dragon shooting flames from both ends, and from a niece whose second favorite word is farts.

SunshineSomerville.com

www.ingramcontent.com/pod-product-compliance
Lightning Source LLC
LaVergne TN
LVHW010118170826
845678LV00012B/2480

* 9 7 9 8 2 3 0 8 2 4 1 5 2 *